Lili Macaroni

by

Nicole Testa

Illustrated by

Annie Boulanger

pajamapress

First published in Canada and the United States in 2019

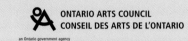

The publisher gratefully acknowledges the support of the Canada Council for the Arts and the Ontario Arts Council for its publishing program. We acknowledge the financial support of the Government of Canada through the Canada Book Fund (CBF) for our publishing activities.

Library and Archives Canada Cataloguing in Publication

Title: Lili Macaroni / by Nicole Testa ; illustrated by Annie Boulanger.
Other titles: Lili Macaroni. English
Names: Testa, Nicole, author. | Boulanger, Annie, 1978- illustrator.
Description: Translation of: Lili Macaroni: je suis comme je suis!
Identifiers: Canadiana 20190075406 | ISBN 9781772780932 (hardcover)
Classification: LCC PS8589.E843 L5413 2019 | DDC jC843/.54—dc23

Publisher Cataloging-in-Publication Data (U.S.)

Names: Testa, Nicole, author. | Boulanger, Annie, illustrator.
Title: Lili Macaroni / by Nicole Testa ; illustrated by Annie Boulanger.
Description: Toronto, Ontario Canada : Pajama Press, 2019. | Originally published in French as: Lili Macaroni - Je Suis Comme Je Suis! | Summary: "Lili Macaroni loves every feature she has inherited from a family member, but when she starts kindergarten she is teased for those very traits. Burdened by unhappiness, she creates a polka-dotted butterfly and imagines it flying her sorrows away—and finds she has introduced a powerful tool for conversations about emotions, self-esteem, and resilience"— Provided by publisher.
Identifiers: ISBN 978-1-77278-093-2 (hardcover)
Subjects: LCSH: Bullying – Juvenile fiction. | Kindergarten – Juvenile fiction. | Imagination – Juvenile fiction. | BISAC: JUVENILE FICTION / Social Themes / Self-Esteem & Self-Reliance. | JUVENILE FICTION / Social Themes / Bullying. | JUVENILE FICTION / Social Themes / Emotions & Feeling.
Classification: LCC PZ7.1T478Li |DDC [E] – dc23

Original art created with traditional and digital media.

Manufactured by Qualibre Inc./Printplus
Printed in China

Pajama Press Inc.
181 Carlaw Ave. Suite 251 Toronto, Ontario Canada, M4M 2S1

Distributed in Canada by UTP Distribution
5201 Dufferin Street Toronto, Ontario Canada, M3H 5T8

Distributed in the U.S. by Ingram Publisher Services
1 Ingram Blvd. La Vergne, TN 37086, USA

To Alexis and Lou…my little polka-dotted butterflies.
To Lorraine, Marie-Ève, and my circle of friends and
family, for their support—N.T.

To my two butterflies, unique
and magnificent—A.B.

My hair is red, just like Mom's. I have Dad's freckly nose. My eyes are blueberry-blue, just like Grandma's. And I have Grandpa's magical laugh that makes everyone smile.

I am the way I am. I'm Lili Macaroni.

Each morning, I wake up my doll Pineapple, my hippopotamus Eggplant and my pirate Petey. I read aloud my favorite books. I make up songs and stories, and draw polka-dotted butterflies. At night, I count the stars.

One day, Dad says, "You are getting big, Lili. It's time you went to school. You'll learn new stories and the letters of the alphabet, how to print your name and the days of the week, and how to add and subtract. And best of all, you'll meet so many new friends."

At school, I meet Eleanor and Frankie and Lou and Fatou. I learn to print my name: Lili Macaroni. I learn to draw chalk pictures and play hopscotch. I listen to new stories. And I count lots of things, not just stars.

I learn about butterflies and moths—blue ones, orange ones with pretty designs, and black and white ones. My favorite is called the luna moth. But I never find anything like my polka-dotted butterflies.

I learn something else. My new friends laugh at my name.
They call me Lili Macaroni-and-cheese.
At first I think it's just a mistake, but after the second
time they call me Lili Macaroni-and-cheese…and the third
time…I don't like macaroni and cheese anymore.

My new friends make fun of my hair. They say it looks like pumpkin hair. After the second time...and the third time...I don't like pumpkins anymore.

They say my eyes are squinty like blueberries.
I don't like blueberries anymore.

They say I have spots on my nose.
I want to scrub-scrub-scrub those spots away.

They say I laugh like a parrot.
There's no magic in a parrot.

I learn that a heart can ache
and blueberries can cry.

I don't laugh anymore. I am too sad to play.

Why didn't Mom, Dad, Grandma, or Grandpa tell me that it wasn't good to be Lili Macaroni?

I decide to erase Lili Macaroni and draw a new girl. This is Sophia. She has black hair like licorice, straight like uncooked spaghetti. Her eyes are like chocolate chips, and she doesn't have freckles—not one.

But...if I take it all away—Mom's hair and Grandma's eyes, Dad's freckles and Grandpa's laugh—how will they feel? If I erase Lili Macaroni, won't they be sad?

So I tear up Sophia. I am the way I am. Sophia is not me.

How do you get rid of a heart that aches? Do you put on armor and chase it away? Trap it in a net? Turn the vacuum on it? Hide from it under the blankets?

Dad has a better idea. "Draw one of your butterflies. It will help fly the heartache away."

So I draw a beautiful butterfly and cut it out.

That night, I clip it to my shoulder. And my heart *does* feel a bit lighter.

The next day at school, I tell the teacher and the whole class why my heart aches and why I need a butterfly on my shoulder.

No one makes a sound.

Mrs. Tamara gives me a hug. "We all feel a little heartache from time to time. I like your butterfly solution, Lili."

On Monday, I am in for a surprise. I see
butterflies everywhere! Even Mrs. Tamara is
wearing one.

And nobody calls me Lili Macaroni-and-cheese.
Not even once.

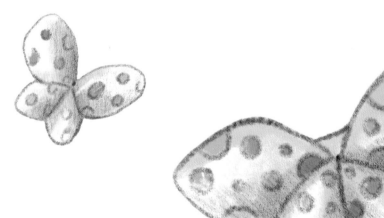

I am bigger now. I love my red hair, my freckles, my blueberry-blue eyes, and my magical laugh.

I know my heart will ache from time to time. Whenever I hurt, I know I can make another butterfly, and some of the heartache will fly away.

One day, I'm going to write a book about the polka-dotted butterfly and how it carries heartache away on its wings. It's not like any other butterfly in the world—like me.

My name is Lili Macaroni, and I am who I am.

IN CASE OF HEARTACHE

IDENTIFICATION: The Polka-dotted Butterfly
comes in many sizes and colors,
with wings covered in polka dots.

ACTIVE TIME: Anytime, day or night

HABITAT: The shoulder

HABITS: It seeks out hearts that ache,
then flies the sad away

Lili Macaroni Inspired Activities

1. Make Your Own Butterfly

Visit pajamapress.ca/resource/lili_macaroni_extra_content/ for instructions and a downloadable template for making your very own butterfly like Lili's.

2. Self-Portrait

Using a mirror, draw a self-portrait. Show a friend your portrait and point to each of your features (hair, eyes, nose, mouth, ears) while saying one good thing about each of them.

3. Follow the (Kind) Leader

When many people said unkind things to Lili, she was hurt. When many people wore a butterfly to show they understood how she was feeling, it helped her to feel better. Play a game of follow-the-leader that helps everyone remember to show kindness together. The leader says something nice about one of the players, and everyone in the game repeats it. Now that person is the new leader and says something nice about another player. This continues until everyone has been the leader.